Can Turtle Fly?

A Lakota Folk Tale

Retold by
Joseph Bruchac

Illustrated by
Gerald McDermott

HAMPTON-BROWN

Characters

Turtle

The birds

Turtle and the birds
want to fly south.

The air is cold. Leaves are falling.
Winter is coming.

Turtle sees some birds.

"Where are you going?" asks Turtle.

"We are flying south," say the birds.

"Why?" asks Turtle.

"Winter will be here soon. There is food down south. Down south it is warm, like summer," say the birds.

"Can I come with you?" asks Turtle.

The birds laugh. "No, you can't!"

"Why not?" asks Turtle.

The birds look at each other.

Then they look at Turtle. They ask,

"Can you fly?"

♪ Can You Fly?

Can you fly, Turtle?
No, I can't!
Can you fly, Turtle?
No, I can't!

(Repeat)

Can you fly, Pretty Bird?
Yes, I can!
Can you fly, Pretty Bird?
Yes, I can!

(Repeat)

"We are sorry, Turtle. You can't come with us," say the birds.
Turtle looks so sad!

Then the birds have an idea. "Can you bite this stick?" they ask. "Can you hold on tight?"

"Yes," says Turtle. "Yes, I can!"

"Good!" say the birds.

They hold the stick, and Turtle bites it hard.

"Now, DO NOT OPEN YOUR MOUTH!" say the birds.

The birds start to fly. They carry Turtle up into the sky.

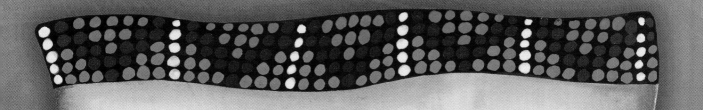

♪ In the Sky
Song

Are the birds way up high?
Are they high in the sky?
Yes, they are!

> *Hey-ah, hey-ah,*
> *Hey, hey, hey.*

Are the birds flying slow?
Are they flying down low?
No, they aren't!

> *Hey-ah, hey-ah,*
> *Hey, hey, hey.*

(Keep singing ▶)

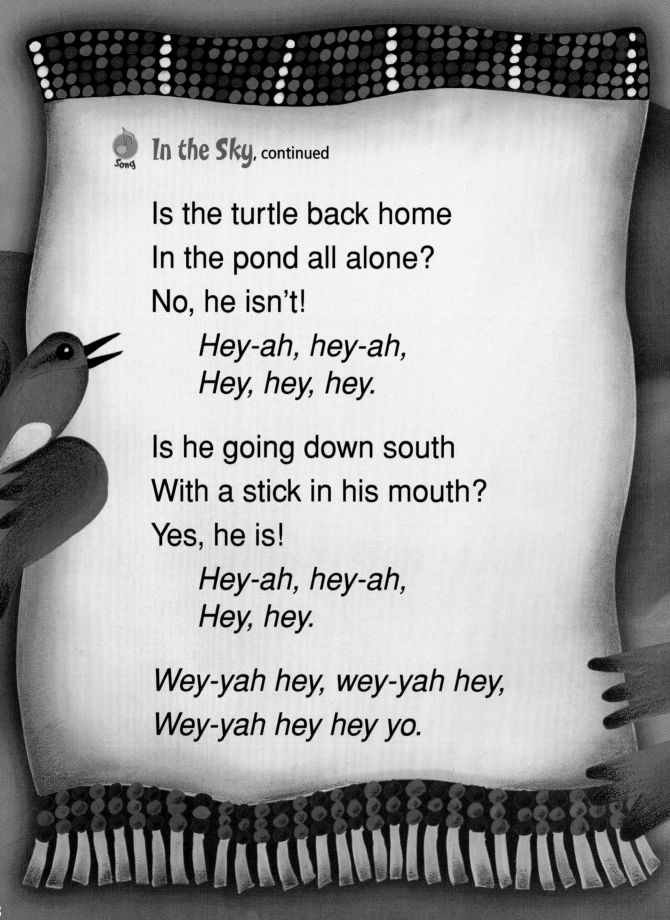

Is the turtle back home
In the pond all alone?
No, he isn't!

Hey-ah, hey-ah,
Hey, hey, hey.

Is he going down south
With a stick in his mouth?
Yes, he is!

Hey-ah, hey-ah,
Hey, hey.

Wey-yah hey, wey-yah hey,
Wey-yah hey hey yo.

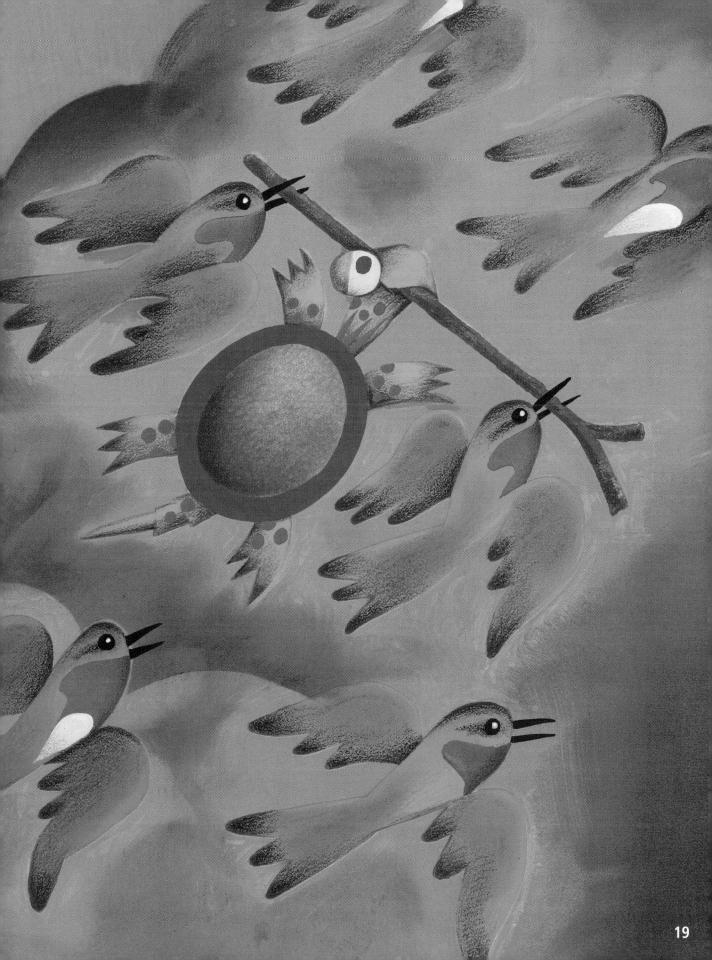

Turtle is high up in the sky. He likes to fly!
Turtle looks down and sees grass and trees.
He sees lakes and rivers. He sees mountains
and valleys. They are all so small!

Turtle wonders, "Where are we? What is down there?" But he can't ask. He can't open his mouth!

The birds keep flying south. Turtle
has more and more questions.

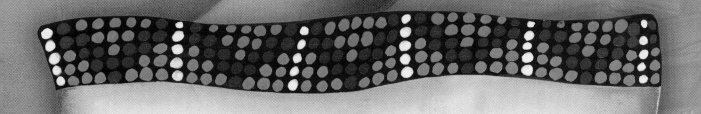

🎵 Turtle's Questions
Song

When can we land?

Who knows the way?

What is this place?

Where can we stay?

Ah hey, ah hey, ah hey, ah hey!

When can I talk?

What can that be?

Where are we?

Who can talk to me?

Ah hee, ah hee, ah hee, ah hee!

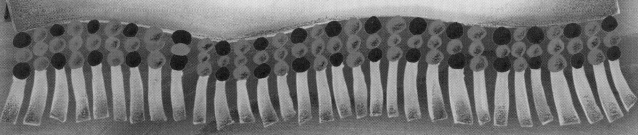

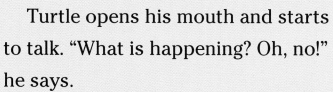

Turtle opens his mouth and starts to talk. "What is happening? Oh, no!" he says.

Turtle falls down,  down,

 down,

 down . . .

Turtle hits the ground—SMACK!
He lands on his back. That makes his
shell crack.

Turtle is hurt and tired.

Turtle finds a pond. He digs a hole in the mud.

Then he crawls into the hole and goes to sleep.

Turtle sleeps for a long time.
He sleeps all winter.

Turtles are the same today. Their shells
look cracked. They sleep in the mud all winter.
Today only birds fly south!